Quarto is the authority on a wide range of topics.

Quarto educates, entertains and enriches the lives of our readers—enthusiasts and lovers of hands-on living.

www.quartoknows.com

Author: Jonathan Litton
Illustrator: Sam LeDoyen
Consultants: Hilary Koll & Steve Mills
Editor: Amanda Askew
Designer: Punch Bowl Design
QED Editor: Carly Madden

First published in the UK in 2017 by
QED Publishing
Part of The Quarto Group
The Old Brewery
6 Blundell Street
London, N7 9BH

ISBN 978-1-78493-852-9

Printed in China

HOW TO BEGIN YOUR ADVENTURE

Are you ready for a brain-bending mission packed with puzzles and problems?

Then this is the book for you!

The Island of Tomorrow isn't like other books where you read through the pages in order. It's a lot more exciting than that because you're the main person in the story! You have to find your own way through the book, flicking backwards and forwards, following the clues until you've finished the whole adventure.

The story starts on page 4, and then tells you where to go next. Every time you face a challenge, you'll have a choice of answers, which look something like this:

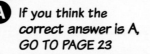

A If you think the correct answer is A, GO TO PAGE 23

B If you think the correct answer is B, GO TO PAGE 11

Choose the correct answer, and then find the correct page and look for the icon.

 Don't worry if you pick the wrong answer. You'll be given an extra clue, then you can go back and try again.

The puzzles and problems in *The Island of Tomorrow* are all about the super world of shapes, sizes and angles, so have your maths skills ready!

To help you there's a list of useful words at the back of the book starting on page 44.

Are you ready?

Then turn the page and let's get started!

THE ISLAND OF TOMORROW

It's early Friday morning and you're at the Explorers' Club. You've signed up for an expedition to trek the islands of the South Pacific Ocean.

The expedition leader, Commander Geo, explodes with laughter when he sees you. Disappointed, you slump at the back of the room and flick through a book.

Property of Commander Geo

South Pacific

NEW CALEDONIA

VANUATU

WALLIS & FUTUNA

FIJI

SAMOA

PROPERTY OF COMMANDER GEO. PRIVATE!

Find The Island of Tomorrow

Inside the book, you find a treasure **map** for the South Pacific! You take a photo and put it back, just before Commander Geo marches over and snatches away the book. Could you beat Commander Geo to the treasure?

TURN TO PAGE 18 to begin your adventure.

Yes! From above, the staircase looks like a circle because each loop is the same size.

Good work. While you admire the spectacular view, here's your final question. Imagine a grid in front of you. Using the **coordinates** (6, 3), what do you find?

What do you say?

〰️ A lagoon.
GO TO PAGE 26

🌀 A baobab tree.
HEAD TO PAGE 39

Try again! This man's tattoo has clear imperfections and is not symmetrical.
TRY AGAIN ON PAGE 17. ↖

No, this entrance has only two lines of symmetry.
TRY AGAIN ON PAGE 25. ↘

You start reading the map again to find your next move, when suddenly it's snatched by Commander Geo riding a snow dragon!
Ha! I knew that old man gave me a dud map, so I found myself a ride and followed you. I'm feeling generous, though, so I'll share the treasure with you.

He whistles and two more snow dragons appear!

You need to choose a ride...
The dragon that breathes snowflakes
with **six-fold symmetry** is tame;
the other is hungry!

The dragons each
breathe a cloud
of snowflakes.

Which dragon do
you choose?

GO TO PAGE 13

TURN TO PAGE 41

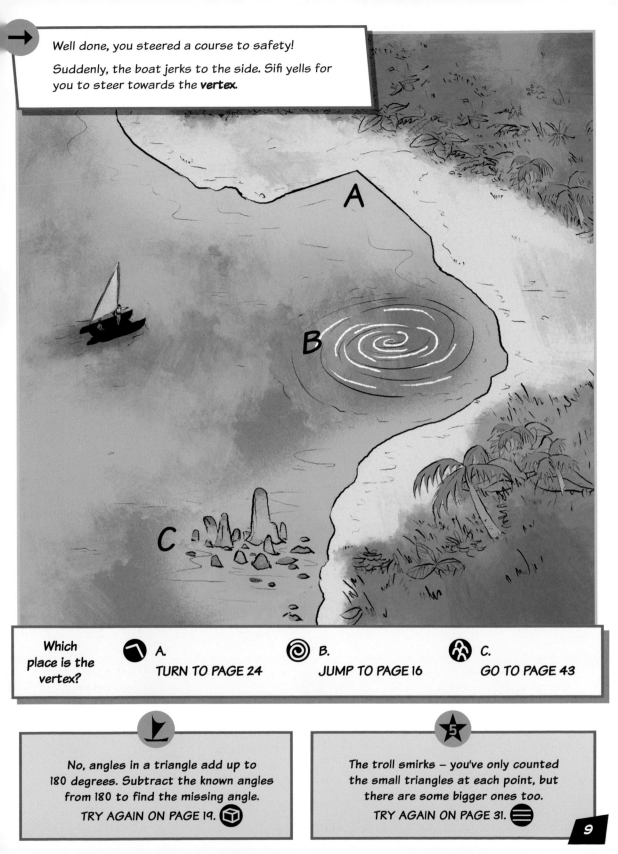

Well done, you steered a course to safety!

Suddenly, the boat jerks to the side. Sifi yells for you to steer towards the **vertex**.

Which place is the vertex?

A.
TURN TO PAGE 24

B.
JUMP TO PAGE 16

C.
GO TO PAGE 43

No, angles in a triangle add up to 180 degrees. Subtract the known angles from 180 to find the missing angle.
TRY AGAIN ON PAGE 19.

The troll smirks — you've only counted the small triangles at each point, but there are some bigger ones too.
TRY AGAIN ON PAGE 31.

Well done! Each side of the turtle tattoo is a perfect reflection of the other side.

You explain that Moana sent you as part of your treasure hunt.

My name is Sifi.
I can take you to The Island of Tomorrow. You'll need to help me move the **cuboids** to my boat first.

Which crates do you carry?	A. GO TO PAGE 19	B. JUMP TO PAGE 26	C. HEAD TO PAGE 37

Look again! There are three lines of symmetry here.

HAVE ANOTHER TRY ON PAGE 25.

Wrong! Use a ruler if you don't believe that they could be parallel.

ANSWER AGAIN ON PAGE 22.

Correct! Scared, you watch the shark with a scalene-shaped fin, until it eventually gives up and disappears.

Sifi lays back and relaxes. Everything is peaceful, until... BEEP... BEEP... BEEP!

It's a message from Commander Geo.

COMMANDER GEO

YOU MAY HAVE CROSSED THE INTERNATIONAL DATE LINE TO THE ISLAND OF TOMORROW, BUT ONLY I HAVE AN INTERNATIONAL DATE WITH THE TREASURE!

In the distance, you can see land. This last section is the trickiest part of the journey because you could run aground on rocks.

Sifi hands you a sketched map of possible routes and asks you to choose the way while he lowers the sail. The sketch shows ocean depths – you should keep a minimum depth of 0.55 metres to avoid the rocks.

Which route do you take?

↗ A. TURN TO PAGE 16

→ B. FLIP TO PAGE 9

↘ C. JUMP TO PAGE 27

Exactly! You and Commander Geo both give the same answer. A shorter ruler leads to a longer coastline because it can measure the shape more accurately.

My favourite art uses an area of maths called **fractals**. You zoom in again and again and the picture keeps repeating!

A

B

He shows you two pictures and asks which is self-repeating?

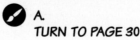

A.
TURN TO PAGE 30

B.
OVER TO PAGE 26

Incorrect! His tattoo may look good, but if you placed a mirror down the centre, you'd see that the sides are not a perfect reflection.
TRY AGAIN ON PAGE 17.

No – think how many degrees are in a whole circle, then a half circle. Then keep halving until you arrive at the right answer.
FLIP BACK TO PAGE 43.

4 Well done! 999999 - 555555 = 444444. The door slides open and a smartly dressed woman comes to meet you.

You asked for a warrior, so you must have the treasure map. I can only help someone who is clever enough to answer this: how many sides does a **heptagon** have?

What do you say?

⑦
7.
FLIP TO PAGE 30

⑥
6.
TURN TO PAGE 43

No, you haven't read the map correctly. The quicksand is at (3, 5).
HAVE ANOTHER TRY ON PAGE 40.

No, this dragon is not the right one — look out for a snowflake with six identical parts.
TRY AGAIN ON PAGE 7.

B
Well done! The opposite side is two sides away on a dice net.
I'm impressed. Now for a fiendish puzzle. See before you floating stones over lava. To access the bridge, how many squares can you make from this pattern of stones? Every square must have a stone in each corner.

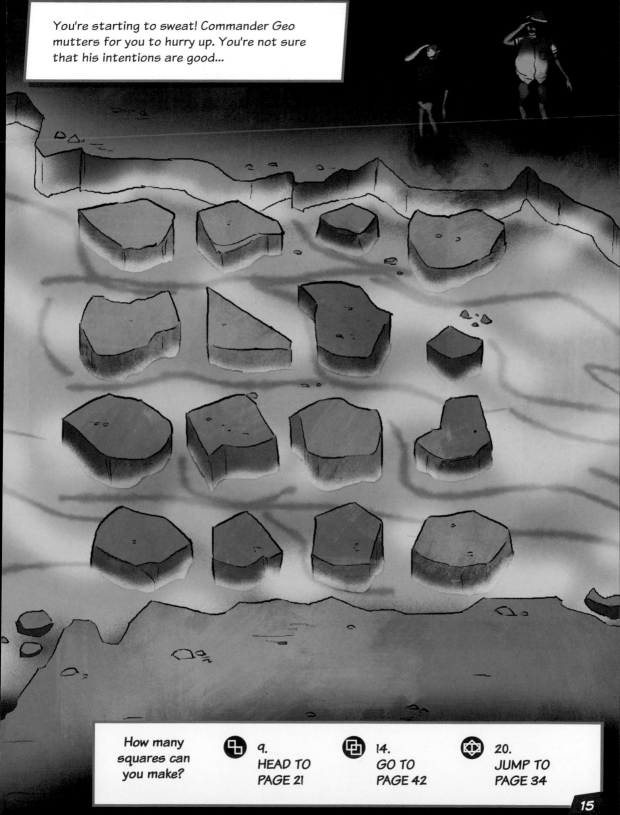

You're starting to sweat! Commander Geo mutters for you to hurry up. You're not sure that his intentions are good...

How many squares can you make?

9.
HEAD TO PAGE 21

14.
GO TO PAGE 42

20.
JUMP TO PAGE 34

Correct. Earth is a spheroid, which means a **sphere**-like shape, rather than a perfect sphere.

Next, Moana guides you towards a staircase, and invites you up to see the view, if you can answer question two...

What does the staircase look like from directly above?

What do you say?

FLIP TO PAGE 5

HEAD TO PAGE 20

No! You must be thinking of a vortex, which is something rapidly rotating like a whirlpool — far too dangerous for a boat.
HEAD BACK TO PAGE 9.

Incorrect. Look again, as part of this route is perilous.
TRY AGAIN ON PAGE 11.

Correct! 45 degrees anticlockwise is a small turn to the left. You walk quickly until you reach a beach.

You spot four sailors, each with a tattoo.

Which tattoo has perfect reflectional symmetry?

A.
TURN TO
PAGE 31

B.
HEAD TO
PAGE 12

C.
JUMP TO
PAGE 10

D.
OVER TO
PAGE 5

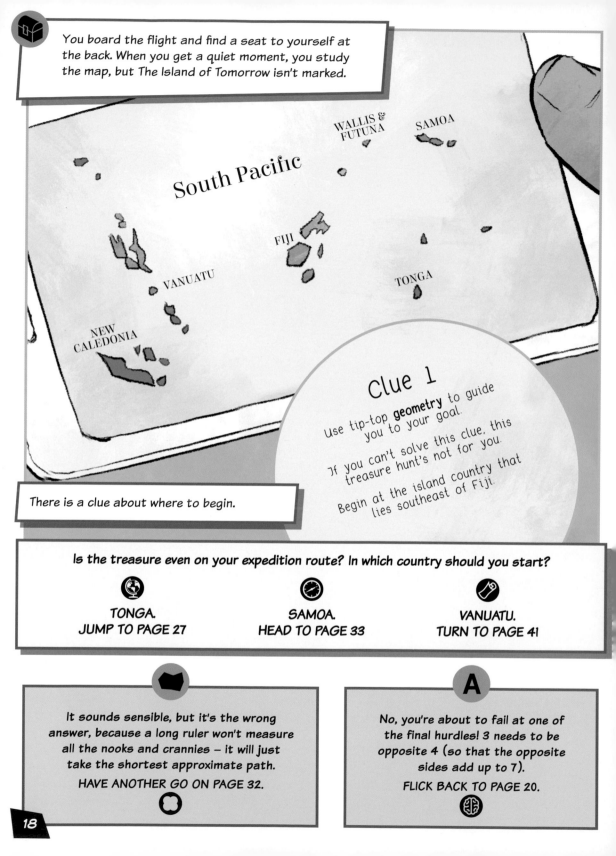

You board the flight and find a seat to yourself at the back. When you get a quiet moment, you study the map, but The Island of Tomorrow isn't marked.

WALLIS & FUTUNA

SAMOA

South Pacific

FIJI

VANUATU

TONGA

NEW CALEDONIA

Clue 1

Use tip-top **geometry** to guide you to your goal.

If you can't solve this clue, this treasure hunt's not for you.

Begin at the island country that lies southeast of Fiji.

There is a clue about where to begin.

Is the treasure even on your expedition route? In which country should you start?

TONGA.
JUMP TO PAGE 27

SAMOA.
HEAD TO PAGE 33

VANUATU.
TURN TO PAGE 41

It sounds sensible, but it's the wrong answer, because a long ruler won't measure all the nooks and crannies — it will just take the shortest approximate path.
HAVE ANOTHER GO ON PAGE 32.

A

No, you're about to fail at one of the final hurdles! 3 needs to be opposite 4 (so that the opposite sides add up to 7).
FLICK BACK TO PAGE 20.

Well done! You pick up as many cuboids as you can carry and make your way towards his boat.

Sifi's boat has an unconventional triangular sail, and he asks you the size of the missing **angle**, to prove your seaworthiness.

30⁰

90⁰

?⁰

What's the missing angle in the sail?

40°.
TURN TO PAGE 9

50°.
FLIP TO PAGE 20

60°.
GO TO PAGE 42

Oops! The troll looks smug and is about to pick you up.
QUICKLY CHOOSE AGAIN ON PAGE 31.

Wrong! There are 360 degrees in a circle, 180 degrees in half a circle and 90 degrees in quarter of a circle. Halve this two more times to find the correct answer.
SCURRY BACK TO PAGE 43.

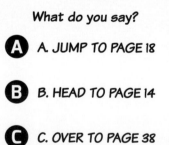

The Volcano Goddess holds up a dice **net** – you were not expecting that!

Human, I have scorched away some of the dots on this dice net. The opposite sides always add up to 7.

A

B

C

Which side should have 3 spots?

What do you say?

A A. JUMP TO PAGE 18

B B. HEAD TO PAGE 14

C C. OVER TO PAGE 38

No! Each loop of the staircase is the same size, so it doesn't look like a spiral from above.
TRY AGAIN ON PAGE 16.

Incorrect. You need to subtract the two known angles from 180 degrees.
TRY AGAIN ON PAGE 19.

A

Correct, a triangular prism has a triangle at either end, connected by **parallel** lines. Sifi offers you some bananas and an energy drink made from coconuts!

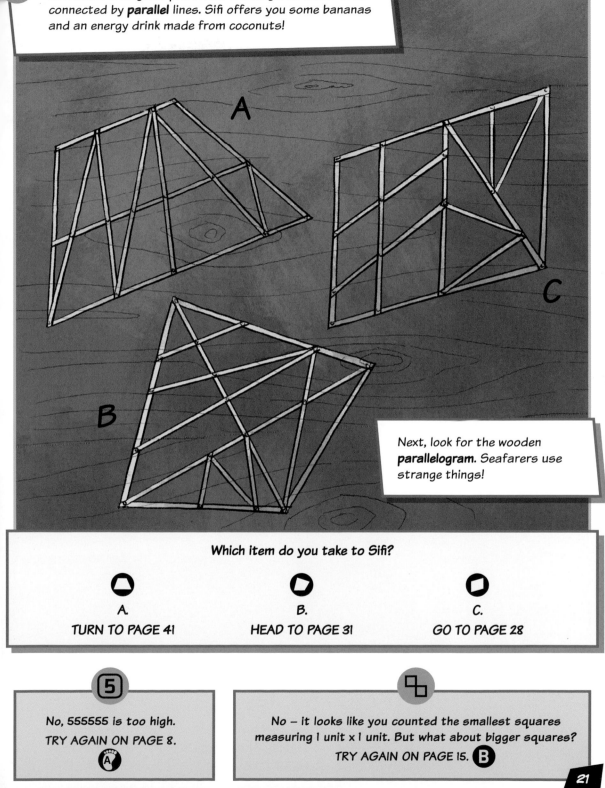

A

C

B

Next, look for the wooden **parallelogram**. Seafarers use strange things!

Which item do you take to Sifi?

A.
TURN TO PAGE 41

B.
HEAD TO PAGE 31

C.
GO TO PAGE 28

5

No, 555555 is too high.
TRY AGAIN ON PAGE 8.
A

No – it looks like you counted the smallest squares measuring 1 unit x 1 unit. But what about bigger squares?
TRY AGAIN ON PAGE 15. B

A
You made it! You're just about to step onto dry land when a troll appears on the final hexagon, blocking your path.
To continue, you must answer me, Fiendish questions – I have three! If you don't get them right, right, right, My pet piranhas will have a bite!
ROADWORKS AHEAD
Many lines run east to west, Your eyes will have a little test. Question one is can you tell, If all these lines are parallel?
He points at a sign. You've never met a troll before and you're not about to argue.
What do you answer?
No, the lines are not parallel. HEAD TO PAGE 10
Yes, the lines are all parallel. GO TO PAGE 31

Correct! An octagon has eight sides and a nonagon has nine. As you and Commander Geo turn the keys simultaneously, the rock door slides open to reveal a passageway into the volcano. You cautiously enter...

As you approach a fork in the tunnel, Commander Geo pushes you over, scratches out part of the direction signs and disappears.

Fortunately he's left part of each word. You remember that most letters are symmetrical, so try to work out what the words say.

Which way should you go?

Left tunnel.
JUMP TO PAGE 38

Right tunnel.
FLIP TO PAGE 8

No, although Earth is not a perfect sphere, it is not considered an ovoid, which means an egg-shaped mass.
TRY AGAIN ON PAGE 30. ⑦

Incorrect. That shark's fin is shaped like an **isosceles triangle**, so won't be interested in you.
KEEP YOUR EYES PEELED FOR THE MAN-EATER ON PAGE 33.

That's right. A vertex is a corner.
You steer the boat in safely and disembark. Before you have a chance to protest, Sifi has left, shouting for you to find the geo-gallery...
As you step onto the beach, a man runs over to you, shaking his fist!
You are not welcome here! Your speedboat has upset the coral reef, and your fancy technology is too noisy!

You explain that you don't know what he's talking about. He describes a man wearing a khaki uniform – Commander Geo must already be on the island. You tell him about the treasure map.

A

C

B

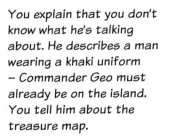

He might be able to help and invites you to join him in his geo-gallery cave. He says the entrance has four **lines of symmetry**.

Which cave is he talking about?

A.
GO TO
PAGE 32

B.
JUMP TO
PAGE 5

C.
FLIP TO
PAGE 10

Yes, this amazing painting repeats itself over and over. Commander Geo isn't as stupid as he looks and gets the answer correct also.

I love painting pictures of objects nestled perfectly together. Do you know what property shapes display when they fit together like this?

What do you say?

Tessellation. JUMP TO PAGE 40

Correlation. FLIP TO PAGE 33

No, you need to go along the **x-axis** (across) first and then along the **y-axis** (up).
HAVE ANOTHER GO ON PAGE 5.

No, the sides aren't parallel, so these aren't cuboids.
TRY AGAIN ON PAGE 10.

That's right! Your geometrical skills are up to the task – Tonga is southeast of Fiji.

Good news! You're starting in Tonga anyway – Commander Geo must've planned it that way.

TONGA AIRPORT

TONGA

Nuku'alofa

○ A

○ B

Clue 2
Head to the point on the map that is twice as far from the airport as it is from the capital city of Nuku'alofa.

A warrior will give you clue 3.

As soon as you land, you slip away unnoticed. You need to get ahead of Commander Geo. The map shows the next clue.

Where should you go?

(A) Point A.
JUMP TO PAGE 8

(B) Point B.
GO TO PAGE 36

No, check each depth carefully, and remember that each depth needs to be at least 0.55 metres for your boat to pass safely.
HAVE ANOTHER GO ON PAGE 11.

Only the octagon-shaped key fits, but look again for the nine-sided shape.
PICK AGAIN ON PAGE 37.

Correct! A parallelogram has two pairs of parallel sides.

This parallelogram is an ancient Polynesian map, showing islands, currents and winds in the Pacific Ocean. But you're holding it the wrong way! Rotate it 270 degrees anticlockwise.

Do it quickly, as Commander Geo is marching across the beach in your direction...

Which position is correct?

A. TURN TO PAGE 8

B. JUMP TO PAGE 33

No, that's 60 degrees anticlockwise and won't take you to the right place.
TRY AGAIN ON PAGE 39.

No, an octagon only has eight sides.
HAVE ANOTHER
TRY ON PAGE 41.

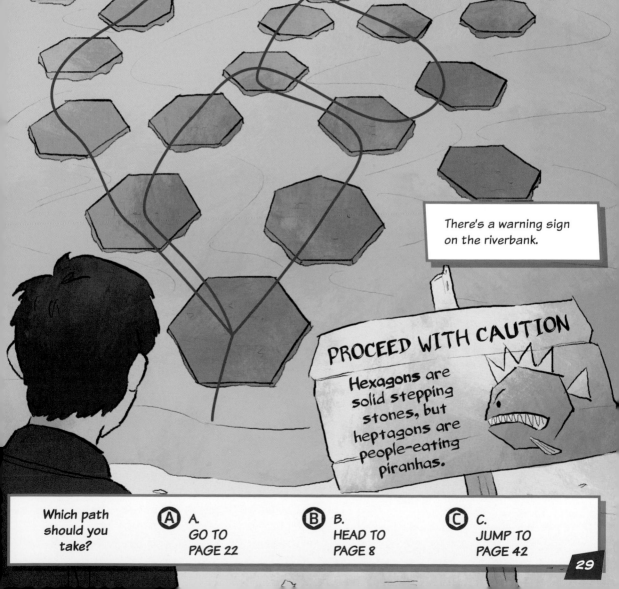

Correct. The river is the first step along the route to the treasure.

Before long you reach the river, where there are stepping stones to cross.

A   B   C

There's a warning sign on the riverbank.

PROCEED WITH CAUTION

Hexagons are solid stepping stones, but heptagons are people-eating piranhas.

Which path should you take?

(A) A. GO TO PAGE 22

(B) B. HEAD TO PAGE 8

(C) C. JUMP TO PAGE 42

7

Correct. A heptagon is a seven-sided shape.

She smiles and introduces herself as Moana, an eco-warrior. You must answer three questions before she'll show you the next clue.

Tonga lies on the equatorial bulge, making it slightly further away from Earth's centre than land near the poles, which is slightly closer to the Earth's centre. Question one: What shape is Earth?

What do you say?

⊗ Ovoid.
GO TO PAGE 23

◈ Spheroid.
JUMP TO PAGE 16

△ Icosahedron.
TURN TO PAGE 37

No, that picture doesn't repeat itself.
TURN BACK AND HAVE ANOTHER GO ON PAGE 12.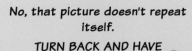

No! Sharks with fins shaped like **equilateral triangles** are perfectly harmless towards humans.
GO BACK TO PAGE 33 AND TRY AGAIN. ◻

Correct! The lines are completely parallel, even though the optical illusion makes them look like they are slanted.

The troll grunts and asks another question.

Count the shapes that have three sides,

Take care because some like to hide!

The troll scratches a shape into the mud.

How many three-sided shapes can you see in the mud?

5.
GO TO PAGE 9

8.
JUMP TO PAGE 43

9.
OFF TO PAGE 19

No, if you look closely, his tattoo isn't perfectly symmetrical.
TRY AGAIN ON PAGE 17.

No, this shape is a kite – pick the parallelogram before Sifi decides not to take you.
GO BACK TO PAGE 21.

31

Spot on – this cave entrance has four lines of symmetry.

Inside the geo-gallery, Commander Geo is already waiting. He demands to be given the next clue.

I am Hanselbrot, a geometry-lover. I will set you both three puzzles. Answer correctly and I'll give you a map.

First, I measured the coast with a kilometre-long ruler. Then I measured it with a metre stick. What happened when I used the shorter ruler?

The length of the coastline was shorter.
GO TO PAGE 18

The length of the coastline was longer.
HEAD TO PAGE 12

Yes! 270 degrees is three-quarters of a turn.

You set sail, just as Commander Geo spots you. He shakes his fist angrily!

B

A

C

Sifi spots a group of sharks and warns you that those with fins in the shape of **scalene triangles** are man-eaters!

Which shark do you need to watch out for?

A.
GO TO PAGE 11

B.
HEAD TO PAGE 23

C.
FLIP TO PAGE 30

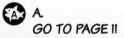

No! Samoa lies northeast of Fiji. Draw a compass with N, S, E and W to help you.
TRY AGAIN ON PAGE 18.

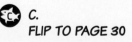

No! In maths, 'correlation' doesn't relate to how shapes fit together.
TRY AGAIN ON PAGE 26.

That's right. There are 20 squares in total.

In a puff of smoke, the squares appear before your eyes, creating a bridge across to the treasure trove!

1 square

9 squares

4 squares

4 squares

2 squares

Commander Geo starts to run across the bridge. The Volcano Goddess instructs the snow dragons to stop him because you are the one who completed the puzzle correctly. They blast snowflakes at him, until he's frozen like a snowman!

You cross the bridge and find diamonds, crystals and minerals, in every shape, size and colour. You choose a beautiful sparkling diamond – a geometrical masterpiece. You've never seen anything like it before.

Not only have you earned your place in the Explorers' Club, you beat Commander Geo to go down in history as the greatest treasure hunter who ever lived!

That's right! A quarter of a circle is 90°, half of this is 45° and half again is 22.5°, which is one-sixteenth of a circle.

Very well, my friend, you're very clever, but watch out for the snowy weather.

The troll skulks away, muttering that he'll have to think of some more fiendish puzzles for the next person to cross his path.

TURN TO PAGE 6 to continue your adventure.

B

Incorrect! This location is the same distance from the airport as it is from the capital. TRY AGAIN ON PAGE 27.

B

No, this is a triangle-based pyramid. TRY AGAIN ON PAGE 42 BEFORE SIFI GETS ANNOYED.

That's right – a dodecagon has 12 sides. Commander Geo finds the key and pushes it into the hole. The door swings open... only to reveal a second door!

There are two keyholes and a message:

Treasure hunters come in pairs,
And here you work together.
But once inside, only one
Can leave with all the treasure!

Begrudgingly, you and Commander Geo cooperate to find the two keys.

The keyholes have eight and nine sides. Which shapes do you need?

Octagon and **nonagon**.
GO TO PAGE 23

Hexagon and octagon.
JUMP TO PAGE 39

Octagon and heptagon.
HEAD TO PAGE 27

No, an icosahedron is a 20-sided 3D shape!
QUICKLY, ANSWER
CORRECTLY ON PAGE 30. ⑦

Incorrect! You've picked up some cylinders, which are tube shapes.
HAVE ANOTHER GO ON PAGE 10. 🐢

A wise choice. You followed the sign that spells out TREASURE. The other way led to DEATH!

You run to catch up with Commander Geo, just as he's entering a cavern to meet a Volcano Goddess.

I am the guardian of the treasure. If you pass my geometry test, you may choose one gem. Fail, and I'll feed you to my dragons.

Commander Geo pushes you forwards. What a coward!

Stay calm and prepare your brain ON PAGE 20.

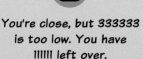

3

You're close, but 333333 is too low. You have llllll left over.
TRY AGAIN ON PAGE 8. Ⓐ

C

Incorrect! Whilst 3 and 4 would be at opposite ends of the net (the flat shape), they wouldn't be on opposite sides when the cube is constructed.
QUICKLY TRY AGAIN ON PAGE 20.

Correct, a baobab tree sits at (6, 3). Moana claps her hands and tells you that the tree holds the next clue.

As you leave, you hear Commander Geo shouting outside the door that he wants to see a warrior RIGHT NOW! You'd better hurry.

You find the clue nailed to the bark of the tree.

Clue 3
Turn 45 degrees anticlockwise and keep walking until you find a sailor with markings showing perfect reflectional symmetry.

B

C

A

Which way do you go?

Direction A.
GO TO PAGE 28

Direction B.
HEAD TO PAGE 17

Direction C.
TURN TO PAGE 42

Wrong! A hendecagon is an eleven-sided shape.
SKIP BACK TO PAGE 41.

No. A hexagon has six sides and an octagon has eight sides.
TRY AGAIN ON PAGE 37.

39

That's right! Tessellation means
an arrangement of shapes that fit
closely together without overlapping.

Hanselbrot hands you each an envelope.
Commander Geo snatches his and leaves.
You thank Hanselbrot and get on your way.
You need to reach the treasure first!

To find the treasure, cross coordinates (9, 3),
then climb higher until you find
the goddess of fire.

You open the envelope and the map shows a volcano
in the centre of the island, along with a clue.

**What is at the coordinates
(9, 3) on the map?**

River.
GO TO PAGE 29

Quicksand.
FLIP TO PAGE 13

Correct. This dragon breathes snowflakes with six lines of symmetry. She stoops down and lets you jump on her back.

The dragons fly quickly towards the centre of the island and the fiery volcano. They land on a ledge with a rock door.

You try the door, but it won't budge. You notice a keyhole that needs a key with 12 sides.

What shape are you looking for?

Dodecagon.
GO TO PAGE 37

Hendecagon.
HEAD TO PAGE 39

Octagon.
FLIP TO PAGE 28

Incorrect! Vanuatu is west of Fiji. Think about where north, south, east and west are on a compass.
HAVE ANOTHER GO ON PAGE 18.

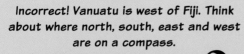
No, a parallelogram has two pairs of parallel sides, but this shape has only one pair.
HAVE ANOTHER GO ON PAGE 21.

Correct! 90° + 30° + 60° = 180°.

Sifi starts to prepare his boat for the journey and asks you to collect some equipment. The boat is quite untidy...

First, find the **triangular prism** crate, containing food and drink.

A

B

Which object should you select?

🅰 A.
GO TO PAGE 21

🅱 B.
JUMP TO PAGE 36

↗
Try again! That's **45 degrees clockwise** and completely the wrong direction.
GO BACK TO PAGE 39 TO HAVE ANOTHER GO.

C
Uh-oh, razor-sharp teeth are pulling at your shoes. Pick more carefully next time to make it across in one piece.
CHOOSE AGAIN ON PAGE 29.

▣
No! You've found squares of different sizes (1 x 1, 2 x 2 and 3 x 3), but what about squares with diagonal sides?
THINK AGAIN ON PAGE 15.
B

Correct! There are 8 triangles in the star – 5 make up the arms and 3 cross the body.

The troll looks impressed, if not a little disappointed that he can't use you as fish food.

> To make the perfect pizza slice
> Cut half a circle in half thrice.
> What's the angle of this wedge?
> Which answer will you quickly pledge?

He magically produces a pizza that has been sliced 4 times!

What do you say?

17.5°.
FLIP TO PAGE 12

22.5°.
JUMP TO PAGE 36

25.0°.
OVER TO PAGE 19

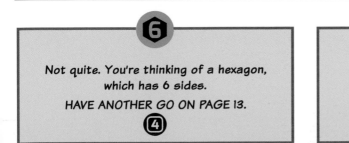

6

Not quite. You're thinking of a hexagon, which has 6 sides.
HAVE ANOTHER GO ON PAGE 13.
4

No, these rocks may rise vertically from the sea, but there is no sharp vertex here.
TRY AGAIN ON PAGE 9.

GLOSSARY

ANGLE
The amount of turn between two straight lines that meet at a vertex (corner). Angles are measured in degrees.

ANTICLOCKWISE
Turning in the opposite direction to the hands of a clock.

CLOCKWISE
Turning in the same direction as the hands of a clock.

COORDINATES
A system of describing an exact location. The first number shows the distance along the x-axis, and the second number shows the distance up the y-axis. The two numbers are written in brackets and separated by a comma.

CUBOID
A three-dimensional shape with six flat faces and eight vertices (corners). All angles are right angles. A cube is a special type of cuboid.

DEGREES (°)
The units used to measure angles. A full turn (complete circle) is 360 degrees, a half-turn (straight line) is 180 degrees, and a right-angle is 90 degrees. The symbol for degrees is °.

DODECAGON
A two-dimensional shape with 12 sides.

EQUILATERAL TRIANGLE
A triangle where all 3 sides are the same length and all 3 angles measure 60 degrees.

FRACTAL
A never-ending pattern that repeats itself; if you zoom in, you will see the same pattern again and again.

GEOMETRY
The area of mathematics that deals with points, lines and shapes. Shapes can be in two dimensions (such as circles and squares) or three dimensions (such as spheres and cubes).

HEPTAGON
A two-dimensional shape with 7 sides.

HEXAGON
A two-dimensional shape with 6 sides.

ISOSCELES TRIANGLE
A triangle with two sides of equal length and two equal angles.

LINE OF SYMMETRY
An imaginary line where you could fold the image and the two halves would match exactly. Lines of symmetry are present in images that have reflectional symmetry. An image may have no lines of symmetry, one line of symmetry, or several lines of symmetry.

MAP
A pictorial representation of locations. Many maps use a scale and a system of coordinates. Maps often contain gridlines to help you read the coordinates.

NET
The two-dimensional 'flat plan' of a three-dimensional shape. You can fold a net to form the three-dimensional shape, such as a net of a cube.

NONAGON
A two-dimensional shape with 9 sides.

OCTAGON
A two-dimensional shape with 8 sides.

OVOID
A three-dimensional shape that resembles an egg.

PARALLEL
Always the same distance apart, and never touching. Railway tracks consist of two parallel lines.

PARALLELOGRAM
A two-dimensional four-sided shape where opposite sides are parallel. Squares and rectangles are special types of parallelograms.

REFLECTIONAL SYMMETRY
Also called mirror symmetry; if you imagine a mirror placed along a line of symmetry, one half will be the reflection of the other half.

SCALENE TRIANGLE
A triangle with three sides of different lengths and three different angles.

SIX-FOLD SYMMETRY
A shape that will look the same in 6 different positions if you rotate it through a full circle.

SPHERE
A round three-dimensional shape, such as a ball. Every point on the outside is the same distance from the centre.

SPHEROID
A three-dimensional shape that is like a sphere, but not perfectly round. Planet Earth is an example of a spheroid.

TESSELLATION
A pattern that fills a surface without any gaps; also known as a tiling. Perfect tessellations use repeated patterns, and the individual shapes are known as tiles.

TRIANGULAR PRISM
A three-dimensional shape with two equal triangles at the ends connected by rectangular faces.

VERTEX
The point at which two or more lines meet; a corner. The plural of vertex is vertices.

X-AXIS
The line on a graph or map that runs horizontally (left to right) from zero. Together with the y-axis, it is used to state coordinates.

Y-AXIS
The line on a graph or map that runs vertically (down to up) from zero. Together with the x-axis, it is used to state coordinates.

TAKING IT FURTHER

The Maths Quest books are designed to motivate children to develop and apply their maths skills through engaging adventure stories. The stories work as games in which children must solve a series of mathematical problems to progress towards the exciting conclusion.

The books do not follow a conventional pattern. The reader is directed to jump forwards and backwards through the book according to the answers given. If their answers are correct, they progress to the next part of the story; if the answer is incorrect, the reader is directed back to try the problem again. Additional support may be found in the glossary at the back of the book.

TO SUPPORT YOUR CHILD'S MATHEMATICAL DEVELOPMENT YOU CAN:

- Read the book with your child.

- Solve the initial problems and discover how the book works.

- Continue reading with your child until he or she is using the book confidently, following the GO TO instructions to find the next puzzle or explanation.

- Encourage your child to read on alone. Ask "What's happening now?". Prompt your child to tell you how the story develops and what problems they have solved.

- Discuss shapes and angles in everyday contexts: spotting 2D and 3D shapes while out and about, noticing symmetry and tessellation in nature, art and architecture, and estimating angles of objects around you.

- Have fun with maps and navigation, setting mini-orienteering challenges in a park or garden. Walk straight for 10 paces, then turn 90 degrees clockwise and take 5 paces, then turn 45 degrees anticlockwise and walk 2 paces, and so on.

- Make your own mathematical art, exploring the wonderful world of tessellation.

- Most of all, make maths fun!